This book belongs to:

....

....

Editor: Alexandra Koken
Designer: Plum Pudding Design

Copyright © QED Publishing 2012

First published in the UK in 2012 by QED Publishing
A Quarto Group company, 230 City Road, London EC1V 2TT

www.qed-publishing.co.uk

ISBN 978 1 84835 823 2

Printed in China

Little Chick
and the
Secret of Sleep

Malachy Doyle and **Gill McLean**

QED Publishing

Little Chick's family were all
fast asleep. But Little Chick wasn't.

She peeked out of the peep hole
and saw a great silvery moon shining on the river.

She followed the
moonlight to the end
of the river,
where it danced
out over the sea.

Little Chick hopped into a boat.
"Maybe I can sleep here," she thought.

But when Little Chick tried
to sleep, she just couldn't.
The waves were too
noisy, the wind
was too cold.

"Oh, what's the secret
of sleep?" she peeped.
"Follow me," said the Moon,
"and I'll show you."

Over the water went Little Chick,
till she came to Monkey Island.

"What's the secret of sleep?"
she asked a lonely monkey.

"It's so boring here
alone," said Monkey.
"I never get tired
enough to sleep."

So, Little Chick
raced Monkey...

...and Monkey
chased
Little Chick.

Soon, Monkey was soundly snoozing.
"So you have to be tired to sleep!" peeped Little Chick.
"Yes," said the Moon. "But that's not all!"

Monkey and Little Chick sailed away to the Island of Fire.

"Hello," said Little Chick to a baby dragon.
"Do you know any secrets of sleep?"
"No, I can't sleep either. I'm too scared of
big DRAGON MONSTERS!" said Dragon.

Little Chick sang Dragon one of her mamma's cluck-a-byes till he was deeply dozing.

"So you have to be tired and you have to feel safe?" she said. "Yes," said the Moon, "but sometimes even that's not enough…"

The boat set sail to the Land of Icicles.
The wind was sharp, the sky was frozen,
and poor Little Chick was all shivery-shaky.

So the baby dragon puffed warm air all around her
till she was warm as toast, and dozy too.

"Oh, you have to be cosy as cosy can be," said Little Chick.

They sailed a long way away,
and Little Chick's eyes began to close.
But not for long – for there, on Mighty Island,
was a herd of noisy elephants.
"Ta-rum! Ta-raa!" they sang.

"They trumpet all night," moaned a
tired little jumbo. "I can never sleep."
"Ah!" said Little Chick. "So it has to be quiet!
Well, I know a place that's quiet at night…"

So she sailed away with her three new friends.

"You're back, Little Chick!" clucked Mamma and Pappa.
"Yes, and I think I can sleep now…" yawned Little Chick.

For at last
she'd found all
the secrets of sleep.
You need to be:

tired, safe, cosy and quiet.

Next steps

Cover the words and ask the children to tell the story just using the pictures. Then uncover the words and see how different the children's story is from the original.

Act out the story with a group of children. The children could play the parts of Little Chick, Monkey, Dragon, Elephant and Mamma and Pappa. An adult could be the voice of the moon. Pretend to sail in a boat, and you could even help them dress up.

Ask the children to choose one word to describe each of the characters in the story. For example, they might say that Monkey is lonely.

Ask the children to draw Little Chick and her new friends.

Little Chick sings Dragon a cluck-a-bye to help him go to sleep. Do the children have anything they like to do before they go to sleep? Do they get a kiss goodnight, or does someone sing them a lullabye?

Without looking at the book, can the children remember all the secrets of sleep that Little Chick discovered? Ask the children if they have all these things when they go to bed.

Ask the children if they ever find it hard to fall asleep. What do they think you need to have a good night's sleep? Do the children have any secrets of sleep of their own?